Published by Scholastic Inc.
90 Old Sherman Turnpike, Danbury, Connecticut 06816.

For information regarding permission, write to:
Disney Licensed Publishing
114 Fifth Avenue, New York, New York 10011.

ISBN 0-7172-6806-3

Designed and produced by Bill SMITH STUDIO.

Printed in the U.S.A.
First printing, October 2003

DISNEY PRINCESS

Thanks, Dopey!

A Story About *Gratitude*

by **Monique Peterson & Kristen Behrens**
illustrated by
S.I. International

SCHOLASTIC INC.

New York   Toronto   London   Auckland   Sydney
Mexico City   New Delhi   Hong Kong   Buenos Aires

*S*now White stepped out of her royal carriage, eager for a visit with her friends. She had not seen them for weeks because she had been so busy at the castle with her husband, the Prince.

"Hello, Dopey," she called to the Dwarf as he ran to greet her. "Where are all the others?"

Snow White watched as Dopey explained. "Oh, so Grumpy's chopping wood," she said. "And Sneezy's fetching water . . . Sleepy and Happy are fishing . . . "

"Doc and Bashful are gathering berries. And you've been sweeping!" Snow White said. "What a busy day everyone is having! Perhaps we could have tea and visit together. I can show you the surprise I'm making for you all."

"It's only a bit cool today, but before long it will be very cold," Snow White said. "I'm making you all new mittens for the winter." She smiled at her friend. "Dopey," she said, "do you want to learn to knit, too?" Dopey nodded his head eagerly.

Dopey tried and tried. At first, he couldn't quite get the hang of it.

$\mathcal{A}$t last, he knitted two stitches together—
then four!

"You're a fast learner, Dopey," Snow White
said. "When I come back for my next visit, I'm
sure you'll be even better. I'll leave some yarn
with you so that you can keep practicing."

*S*now White kissed him on the forehead. "Tell everyone I said hello."

Dopey blushed and waved good-bye.

As the Dwarfs walked back to the cottage, Grumpy moaned, "Chopping wood on a hot day is hard work. But I hate it more when the winter wind blows on my neck."

*T*hat gave Dopey an idea. He would make Grumpy the perfect present. And he would use what Snow White had taught him to do it!

In the days that passed, Dopey spent all of his free time knitting in secret.

He got up early in the morning while everyone else was sleeping.

$\mathcal{A}$t night, he tiptoed downstairs after everyone fell asleep to do more work.

During the day, he hid his special project under the mattress on his bed.

*S*ometimes, his friend Snow White came over to give him a helping hand.

"My, Dopey, you're really getting the hang of this," she said, holding up a length of scarf.

Dopey was happy to hear such praise. It made him work harder than ever.

As the scarf got longer, it was harder and harder to fit in Dopey's hiding place.

One day, Snow White came for a visit. All the Dwarfs were there to greet her.

"I've brought you a surprise," she said happily, as she held up several pairs of mittens.

"Hooray! Thank you, Snow White," they all said—all but Grumpy. He just frowned.

Later that afternoon, Doc tried on his pair of mittens.

"What good are mittens now?" Grumpy said to Doc. "It's not cold enough!"

Doc pointed to the tree outside the window. "Once all the leaves fall to the ground, winter will be here," he explained. "It's already getting colder in the diamond mine."

Grumpy just shrugged.

One morning soon afterward, Snow White visited the Dwarfs just as they were leaving for work. "I've brought some treats for you to take for lunch," she said.

"Thank you, Snow White," Doc said.
"Your gifts always come in handy. And thanks
again for these mittens. They're very helpful on a
cold day like today."

One by one, the other Dwarfs thanked her, too,
as they headed for the mine.

Just as Dopey was about to leave, he overheard Grumpy tell Snow White that at least his hands would be warm.

*D*opey knew this meant that Grumpy was cold! Maybe now was the right time to give Grumpy his gift. So Dopey ran inside to get it.

Running back outdoors, Dopey wrapped his long scarf around Grumpy again and again. Then Dopey clapped his hands happily. Suddenly he realized he had forgotten his mittens and ran inside to get them.

"What is *this*?" Grumpy snorted.

"Dopey made you a scarf," Snow White quietly explained.

"This is no scarf," Grumpy said. "This is some kind of joke!"

Snow White watched with concern as Grumpy tried to unwind himself.

Grumpy didn't like the gift. Snow White worried that Dopey's feelings would be hurt. *What would a princess do?*

Snow White smiled gently. "Dopey wanted you to be warm all winter long."

"But everyone will laugh at me," Grumpy said.

"Just remember," said Snow White, "the love that goes into a gift is much more important than the gift itself."

Grumpy unwound the scarf and held it up. He looked at it carefully. "Maybe it is worth a try after all," Grumpy thought. He flung it around his shoulders.

Grumpy wound it this way and that. Then he tossed one end behind his back and smiled!

When Dopey came back, Grumpy was wearing his scarf proudly.

"Thanks, Dopey!" Grumpy said. "I guess I can't complain about the cold ever again."

Snow White gave Grumpy a big smile.
Then she turned to Dopey and said, "It's a
wonderful scarf, Dopey. I'm proud of you.
You worked very hard to help a friend."

Dopey was very happy that his gift was such a success.

Snow White smiled approvingly as she waved good-bye.

"This scarf is big enough for two of us, Dopey," Grumpy said. "It will keep us both warm. Now, let's get to work."

The End